The rights of Mark Birchall to be identified as the author and illustrator of this
work have been asserted by him in accordance with the Copyright, Designs and Patents Act, 1988.
First published in Great Britain in 2004 by Andersen Press Ltd., 20 Vauxhall Bridge Road,
London SW1V 2SA. Published in Australia by Random House Australia Pty.,
20 Alfred Street, Milsons Point, Sydney, NSW 2061. All rights reserved.
Colour separated in Italy by Scanner Service, Verona.
Printed and bound in Italy by Grafiche AZ, Verona.

10 9 8 7 6 5 4 3 2 1

British Library Cataloguing in Publication Data available.

ISBN 1 84270 233 5

This book has been printed on acid-free paper

For Mum
and Dad
and Sasha

The CherryTree Eggs

Mark Birchall

Andersen Press · London

Tortoise, Mole and Weasel were friends.
They lived near a tall cherry tree.
It was so tall, that even when they climbed up
on one another's shoulders they couldn't reach
the fruit, and the birds got to eat almost all of it.

But sometimes a few of the delicious cherries would get dropped, so the friends often searched the ground around the tree. Then they would share whatever they had found.

One day, Weasel discovered
an egg nestling in the
grass there.

"Let's eat it," he said.

"But it's so small it would hardly be worth it," said Tortoise, who had once been an egg himself. "Let's put it somewhere warm to hatch out."

"Good idea," said Weasel. "It'll be tastier that way."

So they took the egg home
and they made a nest,
and Tortoise watched
over it for day
after day . . .

until . . .

at last . . .

it hatched!

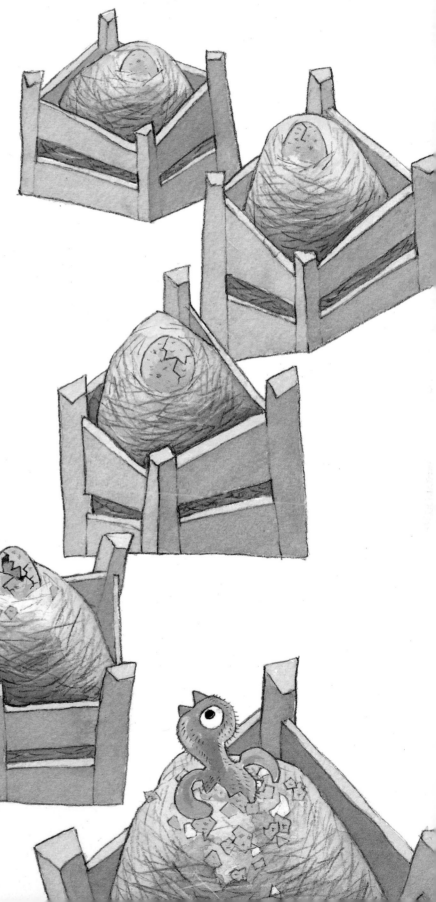

The baby bird was hungry but not as hungry as Weasel.
"Now let's eat it," he said.

Tortoise and Mole looked worried.
"But he's such a scrawny little thing,"
said Mole. "Perhaps I should feed him up."
"Yes," agreed Weasel. "Fatten it up
and then we'll eat it."

So for day after day
Mole went hunting for worms to feed the little bird.

And each day Weasel looked and asked, "Is it ready to eat yet?"
And Mole would say, "No, not yet."

But one day Mole said, "I don't think he'll grow any more."

"Oh," said Weasel, and he went very thoughtful.

"What's the matter?" Tortoise and Mole asked him, hopefully.

"I've known this little bird all his life
and now he feels like a friend. Do we have to eat him?"

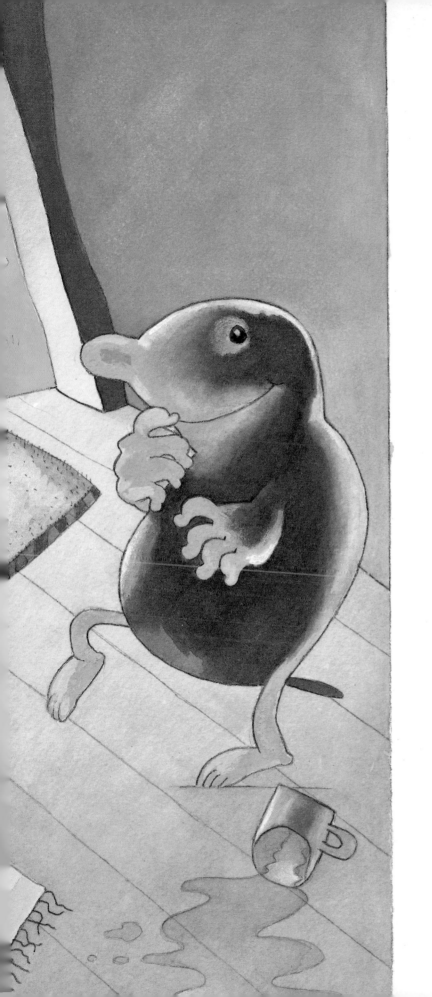

"Absolutely not!"
said Tortoise.

"That's just what we hoped
you'd say," said Mole.

"Let's let him go,"
said Weasel. "After all, there
are lots of other lovely things
to eat."

So they watched the little bird fly up and away . . .

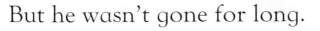

But he wasn't gone for long.
Soon he was back with a beakful of cherries.
All summer long Bird flew to the top of the tall tree
and picked the ripest, sweetest cherries,
and carried them down to his friends.

And in winter, when there were no more cherries to eat,
they all shared worms on toast.
Except for Tortoise –
who was dreaming of long summer days,
eating sweet cherries with his three friends.

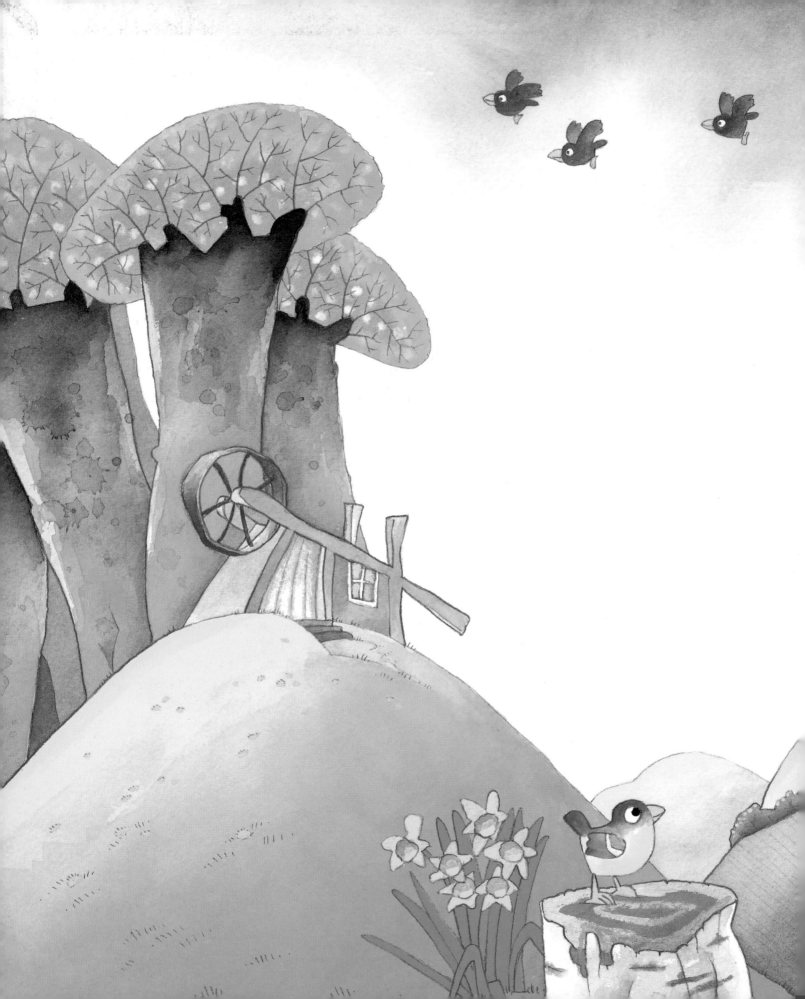